The Verge

of

Nowhere

by K. Daniel Crow

K. Daniel Crow

FIRST EDITION

Published by Darkhouse Creatives

ISBN: 9798581960516

In loving memory

of family

who never got to read it

Contents

Inspired by

A True Scottish Horror Story

Part 1

"And after you have suffered a little while, the God of all grace, who has called you to his eternal glory in Christ, will himself restore, confirm, strengthen, and establish you."

- 1 Peter, 5:10

D oubt struck like a punch to the gut as another wave broke against the hull.

"There's the lass," he howled through the cacophony of sea swells and downpour, "yer see 'er?"

I clutched the gunwale for support as the stunted ferry dipped into the trough of another wave. Finally, I beheld the lighthouse, arisen from a rocky island throne, dominating the skyline with tyrannical glory. The sight of the Lord himself, reaching out across the water—a holy monocle stilted upon a shell-white tower.

Boom! We hit the bottom of the swell. Seaspray lifted towards heaven and pelted the provisions strewn about the deck. Under the shelter of the cabin, the lumbering ferryman stood hunched, courting a lit matchstick to a cigarette. He shouted in puffs of smoke, "Gonnae be a tough mooring."

"Aye." The strange word soured into a briny aftertaste, bathing amongst the saltwater that seeped in and petrified my tongue. I backed the diluted salivate and swallowed.

Ahead, the haar gave way revealing a fortress of jagged black rock that clad the entire island, and the onslaught of ocean crashed against it as an endless siege of cannon fire.

The Scottish torrent pulled us towards the dock which reached out with a crumbling sodden arm to grasp. The mooring line launched overhead. The ferry spluttered to a stop and those vibrations that had numbed me to the cold dispersed.

The ferryman strode out of the cabin, looked at me, strained his eyes and shook his head. I was no mariner or lightkeeper he'd know. Yet to be baptised, I was a clean-shaven face from the mainland not meant for coarse worlds such as this. It was clear I did not belong, a drowned rat, with lips split and cheeks reddened by the sharp, screaming wind.

"Storm's comin' and a long dark nay far behind. Best get yer inside, lad."

One-two-three strides he took to cover the width of the deck. His stiff black wax coat remained uncreased from his broad shoulders down to his boots. He moved uncomfortably close to me and unfurled from his hunch, extending no less than a foot above me with the end of his long beard scratching my forehead, and those tangled grey hairs writhed like tiny worms.

"Hm," he huffed beastly, pushing his tobacco breath to condensate over my skin. I could see his features clearly for the first time, and I'd describe his appearance akin to rock: dulled, grey-hued tones and clouded squinting eyes that seemed far away, entrenched within their blackened sockets—two deep stone wells etched by many a coastal winter.

He was surprisingly nimble climbing out of the ferry and secured the rope around the mooring post in minutes. He lowered into a squat, and from the bobbing boat side, we hauled the provisions onto the dock. "I thought there'd be more than this," I said.

"Aye," he replied.

He gestured his hand, and I took his offer with a firm grip. He yanked me up onto the dock beside him. "Donnae know, ey?" He picked up one of the crates. "Principal Keeper's on leave. He'll be back on relief day with more. Should be enough supply tae last yer a couple of weeks." He swivelled on his heels and stomped away.

I slung my rucksack over my shoulder, picked up my designated crate and followed.

"Ah was told yer knew how to work 'er so," he continued.

"Her?"

"Aye, *her*, the light. The Board tol' me ye'd know."

"I know machines. I'm sure I can make it work."

"There's a good lad."

"And this Principal Keeper, he have a name?"

"Name's Hugh. Ol' head, so they say."

"Then I'm to man the place by myself?"

"Aye. Ah thought they'd told yer. Two weeks if that. 'Er, see, the bulb wonnae need much maintenance 'cept a rub-down… maybe strain the mercury float under the beacon. Otherwise, the lass's plain an' simple. Diesel, see, she's already electric."

"And what if this Hugh never shows?"

"Donnae worry, he'll show."

The wood progressed to stone as we crossed the dock to the island. With soaked soles, we staggered up the steps carved into the cliffside; rough-hewn with smooth lethal edges, the steepness went on, skirting around the corner above a sheer drop. No guide rope or handrails of the sort to grab, I was left only with my nerve and this crate to hold, and the worn rubber grip of these leased-out boots underfoot.

The path continued upwards and wedged us into a crevice between two mightier crags. These titanous cheeks armed with daggers of rock snagged our clothes as we pushed through. Meat in a grinder, we were, as we side-stepped through the narrow.

At the top of the climb, the weather unleashed itself in a torrent of slicing gusts laced with cut-throat rain. I held up an arm to block the attack and forced my eyes open to view it all: The Lord over the sea, the bastion of light affronting the dark and fathomless sin.

We meandered up a rich green hill, and atop this pedal stool sat the one-story off-white cottage which at its front resembled a grimacing face. There was an oak door in the middle as its mouth, swallowed by an overbite of honey-brown bricks, and besides this were the eyes set as rectangular windows glaring at us on our approach.

Above the cottage was the great trident, the watchtower, the reach of our Lord extending into the clouds. To the east, there was a barn, foghorn and a slipway. Southwards we'd just came from with the dock and mooring posts, and west was a rectangle of short walls meant to keep cattle. "There used to be many lodgings here?" I asked.

"Aye, Keepers an' their families alike. Not for decades gone, mind. See—" his voice trailed off into the wind

"What? I can't—"

He swivelled back around. "—Ah said, she's tae be automated soon, the beacon."

"Right."

Instant relief as I stepped beneath the overhang of the front door. I gasped, and from my breath, a fine whispy-white mist swirled and hung to the air, reminding me of pine forests respiring into winter mornings. The ferryman ducked into the overhang and pressed himself against me. "Yer'll get used to it," he said without sympathy. He slotted the keys into the lock and twisted the knob.

I strode into the cottage and sniffed deeply. The place was unkept, the air stale with dust particles suspended in the little daylight that rushed in. The smell of mould lingered about the place yet remained unseen. A low mood bowed with the walls, seeping in through the cracked plaster which shimmered with this wet residue of visible melancholy. I found no comfort from the outside world in here, only a stretched hostility with a different and more nefarious disguise.

The rucksack slipped from my shoulder, and we dumped the provisions haphazardly in the hallway. I ripped off my raincoat and hooked it on one of the two pegs beside the door. To the right was the kitchen, fashioned with cheap pine cupboards and linoleum flooring. There was an old-style cast-iron oven above which hung copper pots and pans, worn and whittled by time. Vile voile curtains patterned the shade of the room.

"How'd yer like it?" he said, brushing the water from his wax coat.

"Seem's... Unlived."

"Aye, nay one's lived here for a wee while, not proper anyway. Keepers come and go. Place has been unmanned past month. Ah've been watching over, but... Now the lass is in yer hands." He secured the keys in my palms. "Lemme give yer a tour."

The ferryman pushed past, dripping a steady column of water down the hallway through to the living room. Here, he knelt by the log burner and, in less than a minute, conjured up a crop of raw flames. The devilish heat was ripe and reached for my sodden soul.

In front of us, two stained yellow sofa chairs sat focal around a dwarfed coffee table, all placed on a patchwork of washed-out rugs that covered the creaking floorboards. The exposed brick walls made the room feel cold, but for some, the view might have made up for the dreary atmosphere; two wide symmetrical windows looked out over the cliffside at the breadth of the Irish Sea. "Yer can see the Isle of Man on a good day," he noted.

There were two bathrooms, both uncannily similar, with dirtied white tiles, tiny metal sinks and baths with basins that had built estuaries of sediment.

"There's six bedr—"

"I like this one," I interrupted.

"Aye, ah bet yer do. It's the Principal Keeper's."

"Of course."

And we went on to the other five bedrooms, each decreasing in size as the tour went on until the last which seemed more for storage than anywhere sound enough to sleep.

Back at the front door, we stared at each other, both waiting for one to break the silence. We spoke at the same time—"Power?"

"The cottage is powered by generator in the engine room—plenty diesel. Check the fuel gauge each morning; top up when needed. Engine itself is ten years old: large K series made in Scotland. It's replaced the Kerosene gas lamp. Electrified now see, ready for automation. Oh, and yer'll need tae use the hand crank to start."

"What about the foghorn?"

"Ey? The Board donnae tell yer that neither? Foghorn's decommissioned. No need in such boatless waters."

"Right."

"There's running water pumped from a spring deep in the island. Plenty of candles if yer want light during the day. What else?" He drew his filthy fingers down the length of his beard. "Nay telephone. If there's an emergency, use the Marine VHF radio; old, aye, but it'll do the job. If all else fails an' yer ne' tae get ashore, there's a skiff docked on the slipway. Nay sure on the state."

"Great. And the lighthouse?"

Outside, we turned right at the forked path leading to the lighthouse.

"Here's the lass," he started, though the wind pushed unintentional pauses into his sentence: "Built... Alan Stevenson... 1843...Sixty-six feet tall...Sixth-Order Fresnel Lens..." I nodded accordingly.

We took shelter back underneath the overhang. The ferryman propped another cigarette into his mouth. Instinctively, I pulled a match from my front pocket, struck a flame and shielded it onto the end.

He looked me over once again and nodded. "Donnae need to watch 'er day n' night." He exhaled that rich smell at me. "This stretch of water ain't crowded, and the light, 'er's stable. Yer'll do fine on yer own for a time. Do what shifts yer feel yer like. Just keep an eye on 'er. Keep warm; keep it simple and keep busy. Try not let yer mind wander too far."

"I'll be fine," I reiterated, switching the little book from my trouser pocket to my hand.

"A Bible?" He was quick to notice. "Hm... No family?"

"None." I squeezed the little book into the folds of my hand. "You don't believe?"

"Hard to believe in anything out here, lad." The end of the cigarette sizzled as he drew in. He puffed out hard. "Isolation can do strange things to a man. Makes light all of one's troubles, makes yer see things that aren't, 'an do things... Out of character. Still, I s'pose it's best yer believe in somefn' if not family."

A squall swooped around the shelter of the cottage, extinguishing the ferryman's cigarette. "Time's up," he said, throwing the butt to the ground. He turned, walked away, and shouted, "Two weeks!"

The front door slammed shut, the cottage juddered and the floorboards creaked. I jerked my head and stared down the hallway. I stared for too long without blinking; until the stillness began to warp and stretch, until an unnerving sense aroused within me. Before I could dwell on it, I pushed my knuckles into my eyes to reset them.

Realisation wrapped around me in a cold and gnawing dampness. It was no more than I deserved. A hard and long road ahead but maybe at the end of it, I could earn my redemption.

I uttered hot air into condensate and whispered: "Home."

I awaited the day's end.

I'd unpacked though not settled. Pacing around the cottage, I stopped at each window and gazed blankly. I was pretending to admire the views as if to conceal my deep thoughts from someone watching, figuring. I became familiar with each space and how every room made me feel or think differently. It was all the same air that remained, even after I opened the windows: close, stale, thick, hard to breathe, and nauseating if I stood still for long enough.

The time arrived.

Outside, the beginning of dusk pressed against the reams of cloud in the sky, and dim shades coiled into bales bloated with moisture. It wouldn't be long before the rain returned.

Like the cottage, the door to the lighthouse was solid oak bolted with iron lines checkered across the front. I slotted the key and pushed, sniffing as I moved into the space. It was a similar air in here too, though encumbered by smells of oil and metal.

My eyes adjusted to the gloom and I could make out a workbench and tools and a metal staircase spiralling up the middle. Under the stairs were boxes of metal bits, machinery and containers. Five steps measured the width, and with one more, I strode into the engine room.

Everything was marine green: the tiles on the floor, the walls, the air tanks and the engine itself, of which had arms and levers and pipes of brass still shining. The large K series Kelvin engine, usually made for boats, sat at the centre cuffed to a generator. At last something familiar, and I smiled a little as I broke away the cobwebs structured between the cylinders.

I pumped diesel into the tank mounted on the wall; this used gravity to feed the engine throughout the night. I splashed a dose of petrol into the low compression cylinders and the carburettor—always unusual for a diesel engine to start with petrol.

"Let's see what you've got."

I cranked the starter motor. The engine complained to the point where I thought it would give out, but it held on, spluttering. I pulled the lever, allowing the diesel to flow into the engine. A terrible rocking noise erupted, and the great

flywheel started spinning. A slow pounding built and built—
dum, dum, dum—on and on it went, ricocheting through me.
It was like being back in the factory.

At the foot of the stairs, I looked up. From this angle,
the metal steps resembled a spiral fossil, twisting towards the
brightness above that managed to squeeze through the inner
seams of the building. I found myself pulled towards it, step
by step, slowly without will or reason. I bypassed the service
room and climbed the ladders to the lantern.

The Lord's light, as sure and stable as it was and
forever will be, lanced out into the undulating cadences of sin:
the sea, and in it, the Devil. But here I felt warm away from
all of that, safe from any treachery or malice. And, coddled
within this fortress of God, I eased out of consciousness...

*...Breathing into black. The taste of sweet salt and then iron.
Gushing liquid, oozing. So much water. The sea, but there are no
stars. Lost. Empty pockets. Fear. A beacon and a great climb. Heavy
breathing. A mouth of light and a man on fire. Skin singed to the
bone. Screaming—*

—At the foot of the stairs, I had been cast out onto my knees. My eyes averted. My head throbbed. My body bruised maybe broken: arms shoulders, ankles, ribs. But now I must pray, "Oh Heavenly Father, guiding light, forgive me for I have sinned. Scorn me with holy fire as I have done wrong. I will walk this path and not stave my pain even though I might be tempted. Scorn me, Lord, and I beg that you forgive me, amen."

It was my own fault, my own stupid fault. I was a disgrace. I deserved it—Heathen Icarus who flew too close to the light. A lazy sinner sleeping beside a fire he did not make. I just wanted to be closer to her, to heaven.

I didn't look up. I remained pinned to the floor on my hands and knees, head bowed in shame. I crawled backwards into the dark and out of the lighthouse. I locked the door tight and wept the short walk back to the cottage.

I needed to e punished so I sent myself naked into the basement.

A brutal storm had arrived and warred against the world outside. Fury bolted down in lightning, and God's rage echoed in thunderstrikes. Hailstones brought down his wrath upon my shelter, and the sea thrashed against the walls of the island with calamity. Hellhounds screamed in the wind, accompanied by the shrieks of creatures from the deep.

I read Bible verses and shivered by candlelight, but I knew it wasn't enough. If I had the strength, I would have stood bare amidst the storm with a belt on my shoulder, exacting upon myself what was just.

Forgive me.

Part 2

"Do not gloat over me, my enemy. Though I have fallen, I will rise.

Though I sit in darkness, the Lord will be my light."

- Micah 7:8

I hoped by then I would be numb to the sound of the sea boring into the cliffside; the perpetual monotonous drumming that rocked the foundations of the island gut hit after gut hit. It appeared as though I'd taken these beatings too with yellowing bruises from the fall muraled across my body.

In bed, I lay on my back watching a slither of daybreak cut the early November darkness, sectioning off the near corner of the room with light. After a short time, its border expanded and reached the mildew that had grown crescent-shaped down towards my bed, causing the damp half-moon to glisten as if lined with tiny gemstones. I could smell it, rotten and stale, like raw meat left out on the kitchen top.

Water dripped close by.

Thoughts came thick and fast into my waking mind. What day was it? What work should I do? What food should I eat? When would the Principal Keeper arrive? After I sunk these questions, my mind stirred aside my senses…

Drip-drop, drip-drop—the sound reappeared in an echo, and with the draft whining, my bedroom felt no better than a cave. It seemed last night's weather remained in part, and I feared the damage God's wrath had done to the roof of the cottage. In that storm, the entire building moaned as though it had come to life: doors banging, wood creaking, wind driving around the rooms in demented screams. I wondered how many more storms this tired place could outlast before the ceiling caved in or the bowing walls gave way.

I slid from my bed into morning prayer. I planted hard onto the floorboards, reaffirming the damage on my knees from last night's grovelling. Fully exposed, I accepted the cold, clasped my hands together and bowed. "Oh, merciful Father…"

In the living room, I sorted yesterday's clothes from the drying rack near the fire. The trousers were still damp, as was the woollen jumper around the cuffs but I put them on nonetheless.

I donned my overcoat and boots at the front door and forced myself out into the foul morning. I walked around the side of the cottage and across the courtyard to the edge of the cliff where I studied the weather.

The morning was wholly dim; the little sun that managed to break through highlighted the seams of swollen clouds on the horizon. Seaspray and mist lowered the visibility further, but I didn't need to see to evaluate the weather. If I listened closely, I could discern the height and ferocity of the waves just by the noise they made as they broke against the island, and thereby I'd know the speed of the wind.

On the war-era VHF radio, I called the maritime station and gave my readings. I would need to do the same again in a few hours and then later this afternoon. I switched the thing off and tapped my fingers rhythmically across the dinner table.

What should I have for breakfast?

I dug into the provisions. I'd eaten a good portion of fresh food already, and only one last slice of bread remained. I had already moved the salted meats and root vegetables to the cool of the basement. Everything else substantial was canned: SPAM, mackerel, custard, condensed milk. There was also flour and yeast to make fresh bread, boxes of salt, pepper and sugar sachets. I settled for beans on toast, sacrificing the last of the loaf.

It was nearly impossible to control the temperature in the cast-iron oven. The toast came out charred black, and I feared not even the beans would save the meal. The sauce overflowed the crusts and drowned the entire plate. I scraped the beans into a parting, creating two tsunami waves along the edges, and stabbed my fork into the centre. The surface blistered apart with an eruption of crumbs. A pyroclastic flow slid back down from their cairns and flooded the crater. I liked soft toast, pale with a slight bronzing in the middle, not this charred black.

I let out a long sigh.

The day leaked in through the voile curtains, and a gentle motivation started to hum inside my stomach as the food settled. I contemplated, staring at the empty bowl and licked-clean spoon, about leaving the beacon lit throughout the day as well as the night. I'd be doing the Lord's work, extending his reach. Or, I would be wasting his light in a time it was not needed. Then I thought about, only briefly, leaving the island to get some groceries or even run away for good, abandoning my post. I could take the little boat the ferryman mentioned that was beached on the slipway. Or I could swim it. It's not a far stretch of sea between the island and the shore. I'm sure I could make it. No, the more I thought, the more I knew that swim would be disastrous even for an Olympian. Riptides were common nearer the shoreline, and underneath that short stretch of water, merciless undertows raced by. Swells and whirlpools danced across the surface seamlessly and silently so that you couldn't see them; that's the true danger of it—deceptively perilous. And, if you managed to pass all that, you'd have a ten-mile walk to the nearest house, freezing and wet to the bone. Save for that boat; there was no way off the island. I was trapped here. But I was being ridiculous. I was here for the long-haul, bound to a goal, bound to God to fulfil this duty. It would take more than the Devil to wash me ashore.

The weather lessened. The wind drew to near nought, and the mist-rain had dispersed. I knew something far worse clotted far away on the horizon, however. Heavy rain was sewn into the brunt of the storm, slowly swelling into purple and black. Tall waves there would be come the evening, I was sure of it. Until then, it was plain sailing.

I went up to the lighthouse and turned off the engine. The beacon went out for the day and would be reignited in the late afternoon just before darkness fell. I pulled the blinds down in the lantern room to protect the bulb from sunlight, not that there was any. I scrubbed the lens panels and, in the downtime of harsh weather, washed the outside glass of the lantern room, balancing precariously on the thin ledge to do so. One gust would have taken me clean off and maybe to my death if I missed the balcony below.

Late morning phased into midday as quick as a blink, and there I stood, perched on the kitchen table, unblinkingly staring at the brewing coffee. I zoned out, thinking maybe I felt—what?—not quite good but… Okay about this moment. Everything was very okay. The day was light, there was no rain, and I'd already finished grafting. The time up until evening was for my leisure; I could either sleep or enjoy myself.

I searched high and low for some enjoyment. I had not brought anything of the sort with me. Drawers, chests, cabinets I searched were all empty save for empty unlabelled bottles and blunt cutlery. I was doomed to a lonely and boring life on this island.

Folded arms, I sat in the living room, elbows on knees, hands supporting my heavy head as if some glum schoolboy. Wait, I hadn't noticed that chest before sat there beside the empty bookshelf. I released the clasps to find only candles and blankets inside and—what is that?—I delved my hands under the woollen surface; two long separate items, both cylindrical. One was metal and hollow, and the other much thinner and more delicate with a handle and a reel. It was a fishing rod.

Rod in-hand and tinned mackerel for bait, I walked across the island to the slipway. From there, I climbed onto the black rocks. There were few footholds between the boulders at the foot of the cliff, and limpets made for serrated edges hard to grasp. I perched on the flattest space I could find, low to the waterline with the soles of my boots clipping the top of the waves.

It was old, but the rod worked fine. It cast, it reeled, what more do rods do? So I cast and reeled, cast and reeled, time and time again. Further and further the line would go, and faster and faster I reeled it in, flicking the rod left to right in jerks to lure the fish—I'd seen it done on a tv show once.

Nothing. Nothing. Nothing. So much nothing that I'm sure the Irish Sea was barren. My effort faded, as did the excitement. I let the line go slack, sitting about two metres in front of me with the bait submerged some depth, and I waited silently, distantly.

Tomorrow the Principal Keeper arrives, or was that today? Maybe he was already here. I'm sure he wasn't. He'd have called or shouted or something. Perhaps he was here and went straight to sleep ready for his evening shift; I suppose it would be his turn after all. Hm…

Looking out at Thunderhole Bay ahead, I could see the mainland; a canvass painted by rolling hills, clusters of trees, greens and browns folding in and out to form the countryside. I could even see buildings, squat and faint, far away: Kirkudbright. I couldn't help think of home. The feeling hit hard too, the mourning of what I'd left behind. A Midlander like me at the borders of the map—what madness drove me here? I had a house; a warm house carefully decorated with expensive wallpaper lacing the walls in textured florals. I had neighbours that knew my name and took out my bins every other week. Imagine coming home from a day of toil, oil and steelwork to the smell of homecooked meals simmering on the stove, made with love and made for me. I could cry, and a droplet crawled down my cheek and broke through my cracked lips. It had started raining.

I reeled in the line and climbed back to the slipway.

The path gradually steepened on the approach to the lighthouse at the most southerly point. Central, however, was a stone barn. I deviated from the main path and went inside, though there wasn't anything to mention: rusted tools here and there, broken windows and pens overgrown with stray weeds. The ceiling weighed heavy on the sidewalls, similar to the cottage but much more severe. The barn was dilapidated, and there was something else off about it. There was a constant crackling—perhaps from glass underfoot—and even stranger still there hung this burnt smell about the place, not like wood or diesel-burning but from meat or fats. And another thing, the way the wind raced through the open front and screamed and—

I turned around.

A sharp chill sliced down my nape and raced down my spine. I pulled my coat tighter. The hissing of someone's breaths, right there in front of me, muffled though faint enough for me to question whether it was there at all. My throat closed. I started wheezing; an invisible noose wrapped around my windpipe. As I choked, heat flashed across my face in waves. Warm moisture collected on the shelves of my cheeks, mouth and across my brow. Gargling, spluttering, I raced out of the barn and gasped for fresh air. The damn place must've been riddled with asbestos.

Coffee again, and I watched it brew as I dwelt on the hours that went by so rapidly; this is how it was on the island. Days, even weeks blew past with the will of the wind. I had slept for some time, or perhaps I'd only zoned out, studying the cosmos of mould growing in my bedroom. I didn't feel well-rested or good for that matter. Even after eating, I felt as vile as the weather that had kicked up outside the cottage.

I'd grounded myself in the kitchen to stop from pacing, and I focussed on the clock. My entire body was tense, from my clenched fists to my jaw. Feet and fingers tapped and I muttered out my agitation mindlessly.

Finally, it was time. I wrapped up for my watch, first taking note of the weather and signalling this to the onshore station through the VHF. There was a storm, sure enough, creeping forward fast from the horizon. Heavy rain, maybe hail I said, judging from the clouds and choppy sea.

In the engine room, I pumped the diesel into the tank above me. I doused the compressors and the carburettor with a little petrol before cranking the starter motor. The great beast started to shake. I pulled the lever to allow the diesel flow and counted the seconds until the flywheel reached its fastest rotation.

The service room situated below the lantern housed the clockworks of the rotator for the light. There wasn't much else except a stool and a chamber pot. This room was warmer than the rest of the lighthouse, save for the spot right next to the Lord above, of course, but I didn't dare go back in there tonight.

Every twenty minutes, I'd get up from the stool, go outside and walk around the balcony in short strides with such a leisurely speed that one looking up might think I'd paused.

I watched the path of light move across the thrashing black waters: the storm was here. The rain hit hard, and the wind pinned me to the outer wall of the lighthouse. Lightning fell in purple forks, cracking like a leather belt upon naked flesh.

In front of me was the great theatre, and I was the audience subject to the discordant terrors of the orchestra —

God's malice came raw as the hunt and as loud as the plates of the Earth crashing. I applauded and cheered from the balcony, screaming, "May the Lord smite thee! May the Lord smite thee! May the—"

Ear-splitting, thunderous doom brought down the symphony with such violent dread, causing the very foundations of the world to quiver. Lightning had struck the top of the building. The shockwave was so close it knocked me out of reason.

My eyes closed. A warm sensation rippled around my silhouette and sunk inwards; a feeling like submersion in a hot bath. Warmer, but I never opened my eyes. The light was watching me. I could feel it on me as a woman's touch. I smiled. The warming sensation drew deeper inside me, centring between my hips where it intensified. All sense of reality gave way. A cavernous void of white light opened up in the back of my mouth, speechless and burning, and everything fell.

I was home. There was food simmering on the stove, and a beer waiting for me on the table. She was gazing out at our garden plastered in a summer's afternoon, pretending that she hadn't heard me walk in. She was wearing the sundress I liked. My lips moved to her neck, and my whispers dressed her ears in silk; precious words, spreading like satin across her worldly worries. That same gravity centred at my middle again.

"No!" I howled against the thunder.

My eyes opened. I was drenched and cold, so cold. I charged from the balcony back into the service room, slamming the door behind me, crashing down the steps. I should have cracked the lens, spit in the diesel or shut off the light.

"Demon! Temptress!" I shouted up the stairs.

Filled with rage, anger at the deceit, I went back to my bedroom and locked the door. I kicked over the chair, swept everything from the desk and threw down the little Bible and stomped on it. I thrashed within my sheets as some leviathan wrestling against a maelstrom, grunting and punching the wall. Tonight, the damn Lord would not receive my prayers.

Drip-drop.

I wriggled amongst the warmth of sleep. The refreshing cold morning rested on my face, softly waking me. That same slither of daybreak pierced the darkness of the room, bursting through the sides of the curtains. The light struck the mould above me and caused the moisture within to glitter against the black-green-purple-tinted background, like the stars in our galaxy. The mould had grown and now reached the headboard. It was feeding off me whilst I slept, off my air and odour.

Drip-drop-drip-dropping in tandem. Two steady leaks fell from the ceiling and landed in rhythmic patters.

I slid out of bed onto the cold floorboards. The scenes from last night quickly played out: overturned table, broken chair, screwed clothes and my Bible on the floor printed with mud from the soles of my boots. My muscles contracted with guilt and lost all strength. I huddled over the tiny book with the droplets of icy water dripping down my head—tears of God.

I wept into prayer, shivering, "Th-thank you, Lord, f-for my punishment, and forgive me for I have strayed…"

My night's rest had been uneasy. Over a poor portion of breakfast, I tried to remember the nightmares. Only glances and reflections of horrors came to me, so it seemed my morning prayers did something at least, protecting me from my memories.

The cottage held a serious cold within its walls. I made no effort to light the burner the day before, and I was suffering for it. I shivered in the still damp clothes from last night. I wiped a sniffling nostril onto my coat sleeve and backed the throat-full of phlegm. Clutching the hot black coffee, I awaited my rekindling.

I secured my coat and opened the door. The storm had passed, yet the driving winds remained, and they pushed me right back into the cottage. I braced against the overhang.

Moving forward with my head bowed, I rammed into the weather. I could hear the sea thrashing terribly. No rain nor thunder to speak of but again, a cruel blackness festered at that same point in the sky, where the horizon met the waterline; an ink blotch infecting both cloud and water, waiting for the day to pass so it could strike.

On the edge of the cliffside, at the southernmost point of the island, I studied the weather. I nearly didn't notice, ignoring it for some moments, the various bits of debris, wood, cans, bags, packages and clothes beaten by the sea. A trail of broken matter strewn and bobbed upon the water, stretching the length of the island.

I followed the debris from the height of the cliff northwards, downwards past the lighthouse. The wreckage unfolded, and I came across the remnants of a hull from a small boat, rocking back and forth on an outcrop of jagged rock. The trail thinned continuing around the top of the island.

I dropped down onto the slipway for a closer look. There was a body—a man, lying flat to the ground faced down. His feet floated on the water, but he wasn't moving. Was he dead? Help-God-think—what should I do?

I stepped towards the body. I didn't rush. I couldn't rush, I was, what? Scared? Yes, I was scared. I was terrified, trembling at the memories of the past flushing into my cheeks.

"Hello?" I said quietly. "Hello?" louder.

I knelt beside the man and nudged. The body was limp. The side of his face was pale, and he wasn't breathing. His arm loose and cold to touch. Still no movement. I flipped him onto his back and started shaking. The shaking became more vigorous the longer I held his shoulders as if I was trying to vibrate him back to life. "Wake up!" I kept repeating.

I quickly ran out of breath. The air was suddenly finite, and I went lightheaded. There was a tightening again—rope around my neck with frays like nails digging into my skin. I wheezed and croaked as the last bits of air left my body. Then, the dark eyes opened beneath me, and that pale face contorted into vicious life, and life wore a mask full of hate and venom; a look I'd seen many times before in passing mirrors.

I was slow to react, half-dead and drowning by the time I did. I was underwater, panicking with his weight on top of me. I slammed weak fists into his sides. I flailed against the stranglehold rupturing my windpipe. I squirmed under him just as a worm under a boot would until I couldn't squirm any longer. Helpless, I let out a final scream, expelling the last air from my lungs into a stream of bubbles that frothed at the surface. My unfurled fists slid down his arms and sank. In micromovements, my fingers desperately pinched onto his bootlaces, trying to hang on to something, anything.

Fully submerged, my blurred vision grew narrower. My periphery closed inwards, creating a vignette around that one sure thing above us all still burning into the gloomy morning: the light of God, distorted, scintillating with the waves that rolled over me. The light had stopped its rotation and bore down on me in a hot holy plasma of glorious white-gold. He was watching. The prayers from a great choir sounded from all around, and the pitch grew higher and higher, evolving into a sharp, almost painful metallic ringing.

I exploded from my stillness and surfaced. The sea burst out of my mouth into his face, and the oxygen rushed back to my blood. Strength again.

My hand clenched onto a stone underwater, and I crashed it into the side of his head. He reeled backwards. We scrambled for power, but I threw my weight on top of him, raised the rock above my head and—"In Salutem Omnium!"—smashed it into his skull once more. He ricocheted against the concrete, knocking him unconscious.

He said something just then. What did he say? I recognised it. "In Salutem Omnium." It was the slogan of the Northern Lighthouse Board: For the safety of all.

What had I done?

Part 3

"God is faithful, and he will not let you be tempted beyond your ability, but with the temptation, he will also provide the way of escape, that you may be able to endure it."

\- 1 Corinthians, 10:14

I sat in the kitchen opposite this man who had tried to kill me. He'd been unconscious for the best part of two hours, and in that time, I'd dragged him from the slipway to the cottage and propped him in a chair at the table.

His chest rose and fell peacefully with each breath.

I'd already calculated a personality for him, and it was one I did not like. I studied every angle of his. He had dark features, and a face of sharp ledges kept with stubble. His hair bedraggled, dried with blood. He was average build and height, not unlike myself, and of a visibly similar age too. There was no doubt that this man here was the Principal Keeper; he knew the Board's slogan, and he'd worn a Lightkeeper's coat with our emblem on the right breast pocket, and yet it still didn't sit right with me.

I wrote the story in my head for him; that he must have set out early morning while the storm raged, misjudged the water and been taken against the rocks. Even with this explanation, many questions remained. I guess he was in shock, which gave some rationale to why he tried to drown me. But I couldn't ignore the burning hate behind his eyes and the sureness of his grip when he held me under the water. He had the keen hands of a killer.

The knife on the table I placed next to a plate with two cuts of rope on it. Every minute that went by I thought about restraining him, tying him to the arms of the chair, maybe even gagging him or resting his neck in a noose in case he tried something. Before I could come to my decision, he stirred.

His eyes opened wide, beaming. I expected him to rise from the seat and into action, but he was still and calm, quietly studying me. He scanned the room, corner to corner, and back at me, in front of me.

"What's that knife for?" he said. His voice was uncannily sharp for someone who had just awoken, with a coarse texture of authority fixed as mortar to his words.

"Just in case," I replied.

"In case of what?"

"In case you decide to try and kill me again."

"Ah," he nodded, "sorry about that."

"You must've been in shock."

"What exactly happened?" he asked.

"I was hoping you could tell me."

"My mind is mostly blank. I remember the water. Nearly drowning. Then you, on top of me, shaking me."

"Yes, right after you'd attacked me on the slipway," I assured.

"As you said, I was in shock."

He watched every movement, listening intently to everything I said, scrutinising each word for his entry. He had this presence about him that was… off.

"You are the Principal Keeper, yes?" I asked.

"… Yes."

"What's your name?"

"Hugh," he replied quickly. "Yours?"

"Robert."

"Nice to meet you, Rob." He grinned.

"Was there anyone else on that boat with you? The ferryman?" I asked.

"Just me. I can handle a boat fine, but the sea is a cruel mistress. Must've taken me off-guard."

"There was a bad storm last night," I let slip.

"That must have been it then; foul waters lingering. You know how it is, I'm sure."

"Sure."

"Have you called the station yet?" he asked.

"Not yet."

"Don't bother. I'll inform them later."

"About the wreck? The provisions?"

"Yes, yes, I will tell them about the boat when I call."

"The provisions?" I reiterated.

"Wait until resupply. Until then I'll use yours."

I looked away. My nose flared with a heavy exhale as I vented out the mounting frustration.

"It's not a problem," he said.

"We'll have to ration—"

"—It's not a problem," he said sternly, half-smiling through his teeth.

I didn't know where to put my eyes, so they darted from dishes to mugs to hanging pans. His gaze, however, remained fixed on me, watching, figuring.

"So," I started, lamely attempting to fill the void, "you're not from around here, are you?"

"Neither are you."

"Where are you from?" I asked.

"Here and there. Nowhere in particular. Work on water and work on land. Jobs down South… And now jobs in Scotland. Yourself?"

"England, Midlands."

"That so? Workin with machines in the Black Country, I'd wager."

"How'd you know?"

"The hands," he commented, opening up his own as jittery as mine with callouses rough as rope. "White finger," he said, flexing his index. It was almost identical to my own, an injury caused by heavy vibrations from machinery.

I changed the conversation, trying to catch him out. "How was your holiday?"

He paused. "Holiday?"

"Did you enjoy it?"

"Of course I did, it's a holiday."

"Where did you go?"

He glanced away, then back at me, and then he snapped, "You going to take your hand away from that blade?"

I put the knife away out of sight and stuffed the loose pieces of rope in my pocket.

"Enough of the chatter, tell me the state of things," he said.

"Right. I've kept the cottage best I can this past week, but the building has taken some wear from the storms. There are leaks in some of the bedrooms."

"We can't have that. You'll have to sort that."

I paused. "Right. I've been delivering the forecast via the VHF radio three times a day and switching the beacon on at dusk and off again as day breaks. I've been keeping watch of her nine till one then I wake just before six-am to start."

"Her, you say?"

"She, the light."

"Will you show her to me?"

"Now? You don't want to rest? You might be concussed or—"

"—Show me her," he demanded.

We rose from our chairs simultaneously, standoffish, and I approached his side of the table with caution. I squeezed past him through the doorway. Our noses came so close I could smell him; as though the sea had puked him up with stale salt dried within his pores.

"My coat?" he asked.

"I'll get it."

I glanced over my shoulder every other step down the hallway. His coat I fetched from the drying rack in front of the fire and gave back to him.

"Mostly dry," he commented.

Outside, beneath the overhang of the cottage, we secured our matching lightkeeper coats.

"Let's see her," he said, gesturing me to take the lead.

I took a step out and hesitated. "Hugh... I was under the impression you had worked on this island before?"

"Who told you that?"

"That's how the Board made it seem."

"Sorry to disappoint. I've worked on many lighthouses but not this one. This is temporary work, they said. No doubt that three months gone I'll be at another light just like it."

We forked right at the path from the cottage and walked up the short incline to the lighthouse. I put the key into the lock and opened the door. Hugh sniffed deeply. "I can smell that—diesel?"

"Aye. Yes."

"Aye?" he snorted.

"A large K series Kelvin engine." I moved into the engine room though he didn't follow. Lingering in the archway just next to the stairs, he kept looking up at something. I went on, "The light is electric, powered by diesel. There's a paraffin backup burner, and the rotation mechanism floats on mercury; that'll need straining soon."

"Mercury?"

"That's right."

"Foul poison, that. Nasty business," he noted, tilting his head upwards again.

"You know how to work this type of engine, Hugh?" I asked.

"Sure, in boats at least. Not seen one in a lighthouse before... Now if you don't mind, I'd like to see the lantern room."

We spiralled around and upwards. The metal stairs vibrated harmoniously with our synchronised footfalls, and I counted not one misaligned note. I felt his presence at my heels like my own shadow, even felt his cooling breath at my nape.

We climbed through the hatch to the lantern room.

"Beautiful," he exclaimed.

"Sixth-order Fresnel lens. She's set to be automated next year."

He sighed, "She'll be soulless, how cruel."

"The modern age of convenience," I replied.

The day from then on was spent bringing Hugh up to speed. It seemed to me he didn't know much at all about lighthouses for a Principal Keeper. I taught him how to start up the light and how to work the Kelvin engine, to use petrol for ignition and then switch the fuel over to the diesel flow.

He wouldn't stop asking about the light, to the point of obsession. After a while, he started to embed the questions within disconnected conversations as if to hide them.

He asked about "The foghorn?" I told him it had been decommissioned, that there was no need for it here. He fired back saying there was no need for two lightkeepers then.

He took a spot check of the food, and said I'd engorged myself without a leader's discipline, said I'd eaten two man's rations and "that will not do". Then he went by each room, ticking off an imaginary checklist in his head, finger testing hard-to-reach places for dust of which he always found. He'd look back at me and glare. My room he called a mess, told me to get to work on the patch of mould immediately.

Hugh was abrasive, by all accounts a boss, but he was company at least. His rigour, this new sense of order and the visible hierarchy put my mind at rest. He was clear, tangible law; physical guidance besides spiritual that rooted me to the ground and stopped me from freefalling.

Perhaps it was his wry half-smiles or his prolonged glares, or his ability to switch from cold to warm in an instant, but there was something else about him that was itching me…

I went right to the edge, to the point where the seaspray rose highest above the cliffs, and I braced against the wind. I leaned over and watched the water crash against the rocks below. There was something down there wedged between two boulders, disguised amongst the seafoam—pale fabric— a white dress, a wedding dress, torn, dirtied and drowned.

"Long way down." Hugh appeared by my side. My focus snapped to him, then back to the rocks. When I glanced back, the seafoam withdrew into the water. There was no trace of the white dress.

Hugh pulled a box of cigarettes from his pocket. "Want one?"

I leant back from the edge. "What? No, I don't smoke."

"Winds are picking up." He propped the cigarette in his mouth. "Can you smell it?"

"The storm?"

"Yeah. Can see it on the horizon."

"Same place as yesterday... And the day before."

"Same place as it's always been," he sighed, struggling to light the cigarette. I cupped my hands around the flame to shield it from the wind. "Thanks."

"Did you contact the Board?" I asked.

"They said *you*'ll have to wait out an extra week for resupply. Understaffed; you know how it is."

"Aye," I replied, my tone somewhere between sarcasm and not. Hugh shot me a glance, though I stared straight ahead at the Irish Sea, at the storm out there growing.

"Why are you here, Rob?"

"What do you mean? I'm here to work, same as you."

He sniggered. "No. Man of your age, working as a junior Wickie, coming here all the way from the Midlands? Doesn't quite add up."

"Nothing to add."

"Fresh start?"

"Something like that. Couldn't work the factories any longer."

"Dum, dum, dum," he beat his chest. "The maddening drones of metal making metal. Dum, dum, dum!" he laughed. "I feel I'm no different from a machine; the same thoughts every day and the same heart thud-thud-thudding. Another Godless machine."

"You don't believe in God?" I asked.

"In God? Ha!" he blew out a torrent of smoke, coughing. "We're all Gods, Rob. God's of our own lives... Do you believe?"

"Yes."

"I can see why. It's enticing, comforting," he chuckled.

"Don't mock me."

"I'm sorry. I used to believe, but I've seen things. There's much strangeness out there in the heart of the oceans, otherworldly things and happenings. All manner of monsters hauled up from trawlers deep, and spectral shapes morphing with the clouds above you. Ungodly shrieks terrorise the sky in bursts of red lightning, and there's that persistent thudding—dum, dum, dum—from the impossible machines far below the surface. I've seen waves the size of cities roll under my ship, and winds so harsh they tear flesh from bone."

"That's ridiculous."

"No more so than crumbling to your knees at the command of some book. Tell me, if I were to push you from this cliff now would your God intervene?"

"Maybe... Yes."

"You truly believe that?"

I stared at him, blankly.

"Lean over the cliff," he said.

"What?"

"Lean over the cliff. If you trust in God, then he will catch you."

"No."

"Then trust in me. I say the wind is strong. It will stop you from falling."

"No." I stepped back.

"So there is doubt there. You doubt your God."

"The Devil's words fill your mouth, Hugh."

He embraced the wind and let it hold him in place at the fringe of the fall. "It's plain reason," he shouted.

"I understand what you're saying. I used to think like that too."

He pulled back from the edge. "What happened?"

"I... Changed."

"So why are you here then, between civilisation and nowhere? If you're so changed, why are you at this in-between place?"

"That's a question I can't fully answer."

"To prove it? Prove that you are changed, right? In front of the light of your Lord? It's very poetic."

I shrugged. "Why are you here?"

"Ah, that's a question I can't fully answer either." We both laughed for the first time.

He flicked the end of the cigarette into the sea, and we walked back to the cottage. We ate together at the kitchen table, rationing the tinned carrots and baby potatoes with a slither of salted meat. I noticed Hugh cut himself a larger piece, but I said nothing.

I bowed my head, interlocked my hands and began. "Bless us, oh Lord, and these thy gifts which—"

"—What is that?" Hugh burst out.

"Grace before we eat." I continued, "Which we are about to receive, from thy bounty, through Christ, our Lord —"

"—Amen," Hugh shouted, stabbing his knife into the meat.

He ate with such a racket: scraping cutlery, obscured breathing, obnoxious chewing. It was a challenge not to lose my head as frustration layered with each niggling note produced. Internally, I prayed as I worked through my own meal for the strength to let it pass.

The cutlery dropped to his plate. "Going up to the light. Wish me luck," he said.

I swallowed my last mouthful. "Good luck."

"I'm borrowing your hat and gloves."

"Sure... When do you want me to take over the watch?"

"Don't bother. I'll do an all-nighter; give you a chance to get some rest." He smiled, moved towards me and patted my shoulder. "You've done a fine job holding the fort by yourself. Put the fire on and relax." Hugh lit a cigarette and nodded before strolling out of the cottage.

But I couldn't relax. I paced from one room to the other and back again. In the living room, I built a fire within the burner and sat, but quickly became too hot. Back in my bedroom, I tried to read passages from my little Bible. The words mustered no meaning, and I couldn't concentrate with the impossibly loud drip-drop-dripping sound coming through the ceiling.

Once again, I checked the mould, as had become routine. Pushing the bed back from the wall, I could see how much it had grown since yesterday—another three inches, positively throbbing with moisture, glistening. I'd kept the window open to air out the smell. I feared perhaps this was only worsening the problem with the seaspray blowing in. Maybe I should move to another bedroom, though the other rooms were unsuitably small and harboured that same off, meaty smell with beds no better than plywood. Tomorrow I would scrub the mould away. Tonight, however, was for relaxing.

So, I returned to the armchair in front of the fire — this is nice. My feet up on a pouffe with toes angled towards the open heat. I could just fall asleep... Only I didn't. I couldn't stop thinking about every single moment I spent with Hugh. Did I like him? I'm not sure. I think maybe I hated him.

In the kitchen, I perched on the countertop, pulled back the voile curtains and watched the rotation of the light. I snacked on dried fruit and nuts and enjoyed this far more than what was considered relaxing.

I wondered what he was doing up there with the light all to himself. I didn't once see him come out onto the balcony to check the sea. I wanted to charge up there and intervene, pull him away from the light, though I imagined him sitting there calmly smoking with a huge grin on his face. "What's up, Robby?" he'd smirk, "you miss her that much?" And I'd throttle him, knocking him from the chair. He would fall back and snag his hair in the rotator mechanism; it would take his scalp clean off. It would happen right under the eyes of the

Lord in the service room. Maybe it would even be the Lord's work, I snorted.

As the light came back around, I noticed Hugh now stood in the lantern room, stationary, seemingly watching me. The light moved on, and I lost sight of him, then returned, this time highlighting Hugh's naked outline pressed against the glass with his arms spread apart, bracing. He was definitely watching me.

Once again, the light faded away, and I counted the seconds until it returned: One… Darkness filled the lantern room as the light moved away.

Two… He knew I was watching him. He's messing with me.

Three… Perhaps he was looking at the cottage and the damn state of it.

Four… Someone like that must surely be mad.

Five… And it felt like the light would never return, that God had deserted me here at the very edges of his love, and at the boundless borders of sin, he'd finally relented.

…Ten… A great flash!

I was blinded as the light came about. A horrific brilliance filled the corners of my being into a blanket of blistering white. Hugh's bare outline, divinified, singed into the lining of my retinas. I yelled in terror as I fell backwards, smacking my head off the floor. The light passed, and the glowing phosphenes that formed Hugh's outline faded.

I scrambled to my feet but hesitated to look. I counted, waited for the light to come back around, watching it move across the grass from the window. I picked a moment and peeped. Hugh was gone.

I snatched the voile curtains to, switched off all the lights and fled to my bedroom. I locked the door, and under the icy drip-dropping, prayed. I prayed for forgiveness, yet I wasn't sure what I was asking him to forgive me for.

"…And though I might be disturbed in times of anguish, please, please continue your guiding light, oh Lord, for me to follow. I will carry your beacon into the seas of hell, even if they might be made from fire, even if it might burn the skin from my body. If this is my road to redemption, so be it, amen."

The wind and rain became foul again and pelted the window like tiny stones. I laid my coat across my duvet, pulled all materials towards my face and shrank into my covers, muttering misworded passages and skewing their meanings until I drifted away.

Part 4

"The Lord knows how to rescue the godly from trials, and to keep

unrighteous under punishment until the day of judgement."

— 2 Peter, 2:9

A clangour pounced across the dark early morning. The crash of all things metal pummelled my eardrums, spawning a headache that drilled inwards at my temples. My face flared into redness with a heat far beyond the November cold, and I whispered curses to condensate rising in tendrils, furling and unfurling upwards to the ceiling.

Crash!

I'm sure of it: Hugh was making that racket on purpose. It was the same unnecessary chaos he made every morning, scavenging for his early morning breakfast before going to sleep. Being Principal Keeper, he'd engineered a new schedule that saw to it he was with the beacon every night whilst I laboured around the island throughout the day. He forbade me from entering the lantern room and kept it padlocked, saying something about me being inexperienced, that I might damage the lens. I let it slide, but naturally began to wonder…

I contemplated whether I should get up. I was already awake. Maybe I could confront him about the noise, perhaps even hurtle a cast-iron frying pan at his forehead. Devil-talk and nonsense I shook from my head and focussed on the dawn of a new day. What day was it? Monday, I knew that but had no idea of the date. I couldn't even be sure we were still in November. Time is liquid on the island, and my liquid was cupped by porous hands.

The calamity of noise rose and dashed around the cottage in heavy footsteps, thud-thud-thudding until they stopped suddenly outside my door.

I rose upright, shoving the covers off me. I could see his shadow under the doorway—what was he doing?

I tip-toed to the door and waited. There was no knock, no hollering and no breathing. The shadow didn't budge, and there came a strong smell of cigarettes. Smoke began to pour through the gaps of the door frame and grew thick as if a fire had broken out. "Hugh?" I panicked, snatching the handle down—

There was no one there.

In the low-lit hallway, I could make out silvery wisps of smoke clinging to the ceiling. I followed the trail to the kitchen which had been ransacked; open cupboards and smashed plates, mugs and glasses, and pans unhooked from the wall lay on the floor. Hugh had found the last of the hidden rations.

My rage returned. I pulled the knife from the tabletop. My grip wrapped around the handle with such a sureness. Each finger found its groove, clenching—it felt good. I sensed myself slip, turn loose and wild. I started growling, grinding my teeth. I wanted to do it, to slice and maul him. I wanted to smash my fists into his face until I'd eroded his features to a smooth surface; until there was nothing left but rubble.

Daylight broke through the curtains, and my rage retracted back into its fur. I'd have to tidy this mess on an empty stomach, but today was a good day. Today was relief day.

I couldn't find the hat and gloves I lent Hugh these past nights. So, I stepped into the biting cold without them, popping my coat collar and plunging my hands into the front pockets. I scurried around the corner of the cottage and across the courtyard. I ploughed through the grass, clearing a single lane of dew all the way to the cliffside. I studied the weather and began to build up the morning report.

And the start of the day was the same as yesterday and the day before that and the day before that, and will surely end exactly the same with another storm. Again, the weather front congealed on the horizon like a scab veined with purple-dark hues, sewn across an off-white tapestry, unmoving. Hourly I'd look up to the sky and check if this inkblot had pillaged the softer clouds. But it always remained there, stagnant until nightfall, benign yet malignant—a cancer on the canvass.

I went back to the cottage and set up the portable VHF to call the station.

"Hello? Hello?" I repeated. I twisted the dials through various frequencies then back again. "Hello? Can anyone hear me? Weather report... come in?" There was no reply, only static crackles. I shut the radio off with the intent to try later. There must have been some bad weather over land...

…Yet, as I stood there on the dock, facing the mainland, the sky was painted only clear blues stretching deep into the stratosphere. There was no bad weather forming over the mainland. Perhaps the poor radio signal earlier was a broadcasting fault.

It was nine-am, and I was waiting for the relief ferry to arrive. I stood for a long time, the heart of the day, studying the sun's presence pass across Thunderhole Bay. The tide moved in and out, though the water remained calm as I predicted. However, I never could predict the currents surrounding the island, pulling under the surface in contrast to the waves. There was a sea stack just ahead of the pier, standing as tall as the cliffs. In its orbit, whirlpools danced in each other's gravity until the lesser was consumed, like some sort of cannibalistic waltz. This ritual produced a larger vortex that had strength enough to break away from the column of rock, cut across the waves and magnetise to the greater mass of the island. The mechanical process turned this unassuming stretch of water into a death trap.

The mainland, normality, was only a gaze away but untouchable nevertheless. I may as well have been in the middle of the Atlantic.

Eventually, I concluded that no relief was arriving today. My stomach twisted in on itself as it realised I wouldn't be eating tonight. I slumped and walked slowly back to the cottage. I hit absolute zero; no energy or enthusiasm to do anything other than wallow. I couldn't even muster the words to pray. Why should I pray? The Lord had seen fit to bless me with nothing. He didn't deserve my praise.

I sat for another long while, maybe an hour or so until mid-afternoon, and the solution finally popped into my head—praise the Lord! Yes. How had I not thought of it earlier? There was a shoal of mackerel clustered near the end of the pier where I stood the day away; perhaps I could catch one. I grabbed the fishing rod and headed back.

I did catch one peculiar-looking fish. It was large enough to spread across three meals with fins and features as any fish has. However, this thing was white with lustre built into its scales that made it shimmer like an oil slick—

pearlescent. It seemed a shame to eat it, but this was a gift from God, to throw it back would be an insult.

The fish tensed-up and struggled. I gripped tight. The scales splintered under pressure, and I felt the flimsy bones bend and break as I squeezed. It calmed, and I saw the acceptance of fate begin as its eyes widened. At that moment, I wondered if it had a soul, and I wondered why God thought my soul was more valuable than its.

Crouched with my right hand clutching the creature's tail, I lifted it above my head and crashed it into the pier. The thing recoiled, twisted, wriggled for freedom as I lifted it again.

Smack!

Blood burst out from its gills. And again, I lifted the fish. It struggled, writhed more desperately as it realised its final chance.

Smack!

That brutal sound of life bashed against a solid surface; I'd heard it before. I turned the fish over. Its head obliterated, and with its last reflex, the thing spasmed, stiffening in my hands as if filled with electricity. After a few seconds, it went limp, emptied.

I carried the dead fish back to the cottage, where I dribbled a column of water through the hallway. I dumped the carcass in the kitchen sink. Hugh was sitting there, slumped in the chair, staring adjacently at the mess stacked on the table.

I turned around to face Hugh. He looked a sorry state. Had he even slept that past week or washed? Dark circles absorbed his eyes. Pale skin and prominent cheekbones that cast shadows underneath so clear-cut they resembled two symmetrical tenches, stretching to his beard line. The consistent tremor of his splayed hands was obvious, and he hunched over as though his spine had given up.

"The relief ferry never came," I started.

"Oh," he sighed.

"And the radio has stopped working."

"Really?"

79

"You didn't know it was broken?" I asked.

"It was fine last time I checked."

"Which was when?"

He shrugged. "Yesterday afternoon, Friday, I suppose, for my weather report."

"Yesterday was Sunday. Today is Monday." I spoke with certainty, but as I did, doubt reaped across my mind.

"That so? The days blur together out here, don't they?"

"We need more supplies, Hugh… Did you even call the Board?"

Now he was looking at me. "For a man obsessed with faith, I thought you'd have more of it."

My fists clenched. "I can't trust a lying man, not here, not anywhere."

"But you'd trust that lying book?" Something about the way he said it, with the usual smirk but a new note of sharpness, hooked in my mouth and pulled the gums from me so I couldn't reply with words, only with action. I was wild and random, out of water, no better than that fish.

I grabbed him by the scruff and—

"—All right! I'll—get off me—I'll sort it."

I let go of him and stepped back, venting my rage with a loud huff.

He returned to his glum hunch at the table. "I'll take the skiff out tomorrow, fetch the supplies."

"I'll take the night watch then, leave you to get some rest," I said.

"You've been awake all day. You'll fall asleep."

"I can handle it."

"You won't have it in you."

"I can handle it," I said sternly.

His jaw clenched, frowning, with his own fists now tightened by his side. I saw the emotion pulse through him. But he didn't have the stomach for it, and I'm not sure I did either. "Aye. Stay in the service room. No need for you to go up to the beacon, understand?"

"Sure."

"Not while the light is on. Don't want you blinding yourself. Don't want you touching the lens neither; she's fragile."

"I'll stay in the service room."

"Good. Now, you best be sharing that fish. We both need our strength for tomorrow."

"I—"

He interrupted, "I'll need some food in me if I'm to make that distance tomorrow. You know how those waters are. It'll be tough rowing that skiff... Boss's orders."

"Sure," I replied.

"You're a good man, Robert. A good man."

I filleted the fish into thin pieces which I pan-fried with the last of the oil. I'd arranged two steaks each, and what remained I wrapped up for breakfast. It was disheartening how quickly the food went down—a skeleton meal for skeleton men.

"Robert," Hugh began audibly and visibly brighter after eating.

I threw the last chunk of fish into my mouth and let it melt on my tongue before replying. "Hm?"

"You didn't say grace."

"Did I not?"

"No."

"Easy mistake to make. I will pray later. Sorry."

"Don't be. You caught that fish, not God."

"But the Lord blessed me with the eyes to see it, the chance to catch it and the strength to pull it out of the water. Plenty to be thankful for."

"It still took mind on your part, no? It took your own skill and patience."

"He blessed me with these traits."

"Goddamn it, Rob," he threw his hands in the air, "you won't even take pride in this?"

"Pride is a sin."

"Then by God, if he did not like sinning, why'd he make it possible?"

"Sin is nothing to do with God. It is a human failure to achieve perfection brought about by the Devil's work," I said.

"Yet God sins all the time, yes? In his wrath, his plagues, his disasters." Within Hugh's words, the agenda started to manifest; in how they were crafted and delivered with such severe sureness, positing himself as sound logic and everything other than his truths was "sheer madness."

"God is perfect in all ways. He cannot sin by definition."

He pulled back in his chair, softening his tone, "Seems a bit hypocritical to me," and he let that notion linger in the space between us. He stared at me, but I couldn't look at him. I didn't know how to reply. I wasn't mad at his heathen outcry, I understood it. I even recognised the words he spoke as though they were my own.

"What's your story, Rob?" Hugh asked, raising an eyebrow.

"What? What story?"

He leant forward, scrunching his eyes into focus. "I can see it's weathered you; your history, your secret."

"What are you talking about? There's no secret." I reclined into my chair, sinking my hands below the table and into my pockets.

"I've seen plenty like you; Keeper's burdened with their past. It lingers about them like cologne. I smell it on you too—that same shallow rot."

"I don't have a secret," I replied.

"C'mon. That's why you're really here, isn't it?"

"I've already told you why I am here: to prove I have changed, to find peace."

"Peace from what, your past sins?" he sneered. "You know, I've seen you stroking that book like it's your damn lover. Who did it belong to?"

I clutched the book in my pocket. "No one. It belongs to me."

Hugh pressed, "It's an old thing. Means someone gave it to you." He gasped as he realised he was "getting warmer? Must have belonged to someone special, perhaps your mother? No?" He scanned the atmosphere around me, studying the subtle changes of energy leaking out through my body language. He was decoding me. "Of course not. Someone else, someone you disappointed or even hurt. That's why you hold it so, yes like that, with that exact face: forlorn, constantly, like a widow in grief." He leant further, elbows on the table with his hands crawling towards me. His focus narrowed, lancing for my centre. "What did you do, Robert?"

"What? N-nothing," my voice raised in a stutter. I could feel it, the implosion, the gradual collapse. My stomach clenched and loosened with each erratic breath. It felt as if my innards were scrapping against the points of my ribcage as they constricted. The emotion began to drool out of me, seeping in salt-streams from my eyes, collecting around my nostrils and stinging my chapped lips where the bitter taste inserted itself into my mouth.

"It's burrowed into you, this secret. It's eating you from the inside-out. Open up. Let it out. I'm your priest, and this is your confession."

"It's nothing. It's—"

"—Confess. This is the first step."

I couldn't make out if he was laughing as he sat there, taunting me, prying me open bit by bit. I, the clam, and he the hunter carefully shuckling his way to the pearl. Only this pearl wasn't beautiful or precious; it was cancerous, it was the pestilent mould on the wall slowly festering, and still, he worked for it, salivating at the thought of my secret, hunting the relief of it as if this were his own poison.

"I've nothing to confess," I said.

He whacked the table. "Confess."

"I can't, I—"

"—Confess!" he smacked the table again. "Confess. Confess. Confess. Confess!"

I slammed my fists, and the force threw me up from my seat.

"I killed her!"

A dam somewhere burst. Freezing water rushed through every crevice and toppled over the verge. The frozen caps of mountains turned to steam, and the over-boiled kettle stopped screaming. Clocks started ticking again, and lockboxes swung open in a symphony of metallic whines. Fresh, fresh air and somewhere far away in the distance, church bells chimed, and birds were singing.

He stared back at me so intensely, changed all of a sudden in this great revelation. If I couldn't see his face, I would have sworn he was smiling. "What was her name?"

"My wife… her name was," I paused. Had I forgotten her name? It hadn't been more than three years. I can't have forgotten. No, it was just buried deep down inside me, entombed by the vast nothingness of daily memories from there and between; a noisy haze created to drown her out. But there's no denying the screams that rippled through the nethermost chasms of my being.

"Her name was Alina." And as I spoke it, I wept.

"How did it happen?" he asked.

"It was an accident. She was… unfaithful. She said she wasn't, that I had to trust her, but I knew. I had her against the wall… I was shaking her mindlessly—no thought just rage—my hands around her delicate neck. She didn't fight. She didn't cry. Maybe she wanted me to do it. Our ship had been sinking for some time: arguments, debts, mortgage… And in the end, she drowned in it all, sunk right down to the very depths of the lake where nobody could find her." I wiped the tears with my sleeve. "But the worst part of it? People felt sorry for me."

"…So you turned to religion, to that Bible of yours."

"It was her's."

"The book that promises forgiveness no matter the sin."

"Book of Mathew twelve-thirty-one: And so I tell you, any sin and blasphemy can be forgiven, but the blasphemy against the Spirit will not be," I recited.

He shook his head. "So that's why you are here? To tend God's light at the edge of the world, at the end of reason. To suffer in front of the Lord's eyes, in front of *her* eyes."

I stayed quiet.

"Do you think that's enough? For forgiveness?" he questioned.

"As long as I stay faithful, perhaps... Well, that's for God to decide, not me."

He tapped his fingers rhythmically across the dinner table. "What if it wasn't. What if there's another option?"

"There is no other option."

"Yes, there is. I've taken it myself."

"What?" I asked boyishly.

He grinned. "Your faith is your weakness. Find strength within, not some ancient words on a page. Take control. Forgive yourself and move on."

"I've not yet earned it."

"You said so yourself you've changed. You've no need for God's forgiveness. If you're waiting for him, I'm afraid you'll be waiting for a long time. Escape his clutches, free yourself. Condemn the book. Or… you can continue to sink… down and down into the depths of self-annihilation, your existence nothing but whalefall of which your sins to feed — drowned like *her*. Forgive yourself. Condemn your Lord."

I hissed, "Devil-talk!"

"If the Devil is the path to survival, then so be it."

"And a certain path to Hell when my reckoning comes."

"Otherwise, you're so certain you'll make it to heaven?" he tutted. "There's no guarantee of forgiveness. You will only know your fate when you are at the foot of those gates."

"Blasphemy is the only unforgivable sin, Hugh. God would only punish me for it."

"Then, God is only a reflection of the Devil, and he does not deserve your praise, and you do not need his forgiveness."

Hugh finally relented, moved his arms from the table, rubbing his hands together as if to dust them off. "Sorry, I don't mean to poke. I used to believe a long time ago. But I'm better now, truly. I accept myself, my history, and I accept that I am changed. I've moved on, and I live. That's what a good God would want for his children."

My head collapsed into my hands. My shoulders rolled forward, and I sat at the table hunched. Only minutes ago, it was Hugh who seemed broken, now look at me; thrown overboard, shipwrecked somewhere betwixt believing and not. Doubt besieged the walls I had built, and I realised that these walls were made from firewood set within a foundation of sand.

"Automation is coming soon," Hugh said. "They wouldn't let you wait out your many many days here anyway. So what's the plan, Rob? Quick bit of prayer, suffer through some hard labour, and then you're forgiven? No, what you are after cannot be achieved. It cannot be given by anyone but yourself."

"Please, just stop talking." Because Hugh's words were whispers from a snake, slippery with cunning and balanced with reason, it was impossible to discern whether he really meant well for me or whether he was gunning for something else—for me to join him in sin and Bible bashing. Whatever he was after, I didn't want to listen to it anymore.

My vision turned blurry, and I put my hand to my head in an overt display of agony. The throbbing migraine that had been humming in the background suddenly became present and impossible to ignore.

"You all right?" Hugh asked.

"My head," I winced.

"Reason can cut deep into one's beliefs."

"It isn't that it's... I've been having a lot of headaches recently."

"So have I. I suspect it's the change in air pressure as we move into winter. Nothing to worry about," he dismissed. "Will you be sound enough to watch the light? I can do it for you."

"I'll be fine."

"Well," Hugh stood from his chair, "I'll take a look at the VHF radio, see if I can contact the Board. I'll tell them I'm coming to shore tomorrow for supplies. Oh, and... You'll feel better."

"It's nothing, just a headache."

"No, I meant the burden. It'll be hard, but if you choose to forgive yourself, it will only get better. Trust me," he said with a smile before striding out.

I didn't trust him though, not even after I'd opened up and spewed my history like guts across his lap. I felt as though I gave him the metaphorical gun I was going to use to conclude all of this, putting it right in his hands for him to decide.

Outside, the world was on the eve of darkness. I hurried up the path to the lighthouse. The driving winds started up already with a ferocity greater than any of the previous nights. The rain began, and the doom of thunder echoed not too far away, flashing in fiery white through the reams of black cloud. Yes, the great storm front had amassed into something much bigger and had dislodged from the horizon. It was gliding across the sky, reflected in the water beneath it, which shimmered with the pale early moonlight; this image would not last, however, as the clouds sprawled across the roof of the world. The countdown started, and the ripe smell of the storm filled my nose. It was the smell of ozone; a sweet zing which stuck to the air like perfume and an early warning of what was to come.

I paced to the engine room, pumped the diesel into the tank above me, doused the carburettor with petrol and hand-cranked the starter motor until the whole engine shook. I snatched the lever over to engage the diesel flow, then climbed up the stairs to the balcony.

I watched the sky turn. The atmosphere flashed with an incandescent blaze that set alight the evening in holy fire. Then the world exploded with momentary colour as the day slipped behind the canvas of the planet. Surreal arches of turquoise bowed down from naked sky, twisting between the valleys of stars, beset by layers of brilliant pinks and greens; neon interlaced within clouds, forming a pattern like fish scales, stretching towards the lighthouse.

Undeniable—I could now perceive the immensity of the storm ahead, clotting the entire horizon, bleeding its darkness into the waterline beneath. But the more I studied the storm, the more it didn't seem right. Apart from the lightning that ran through it, the shroud seemed to bloat and swell as if it were living, breathing matter. Appendages of cloud, tentacles, extended from the pulsating mass and quickly inked everything to obsidian; night bleached the painting.

The storm had arrived.

With elbows resting on the railing, I interlocked my fingers ready for prayer. "Wrathful Lord, I beg for—" I stopped short. I meant in my mind to say it, yet the words did not follow. My hands broke away from one another and clenched into fists. "Lord," I began. I hammered on the railing and repeated through gritted teeth, "Lord I—"

In the service room next to the beacon's rotator, I pulled the mercury straining rag from the back of the chair and stuffed it into my pocket. I sat holding the little Bible in my hands. I didn't open it. I only studied the front cover, tracing a fingertip around the golden lettering.

I realised my own hands were shaking as badly as Hugh's were. Working on the machines as I did, it was normal to have hands that tremored, pain in the wrists which always seemed to worsen come winter. That's all it was, nothing more.

The storm hit the island, and I felt content cosied into my coat. The cold would occasionally hike up my ankles or abseil down my nape, causing the hairs to stand on end. I took some small amount of pleasure from the sensation and, for the first time on that island, I relaxed. A great war raged outside—the howls of the tempest and its discordant destruction. I could hear the rattle of loose tarpaulin that had lost one of its moorings, and the racket of sheet metal denting inwards from the force of the wind, the shattering of glass, the bending and snapping of wood and the constant creaking of the lighthouse itself.

Hours went by slowly, or quickly, I couldn't tell. Consciousness oscillated through peaks and troughs, of exhaustion, activity and not, standing and sitting, there but not really there. At some point, my hands got so cold that the sensation of touch left me, as did my wife's Bible, which slipped from my grip and fell down the metal stairs in staggered dulcet chimes.

Every time boredom struck, I had a go at the padlocked hatch that kept me from the lantern room. One time I tried with a spanner, the other with a wrench, but the padlock didn't come loose. I obsessed about it, loitering at the bottom of the ladder when I wasn't sitting. I swear I could hear the faint sweet humming of a woman's voice, *her* voice, although

I knew that was not possible. The charming tone was just another note of the storm's symphony.

Another hour went by, or was it only minutes?

Then, everything went black—

Lights out!

And, I tried to open my eyes that were not closed. I was no longer sitting but walking aimlessly forward into the unknown, into the critical cold. Every step I feared a great fall that never came.

I collided with a railing of which my hands desperately clung to. I anchored myself as the severe winds surged with gusts that sought to carry me off into nowhere, perhaps to heaven, perhaps to my judgement. Perhaps I should have let go.

I was on the balcony of the lighthouse amidst the heart of the storm. I was no longer wearing a coat. I wasn't wearing any clothes. Completely bare, prepped for the hail-razors to dash about my skin and God's whip to tear the flesh from my back as thunder struck.

Finally, a light pierced through the wretched darkness to guide me. "Oh, thank you, Lord. Merciful God," I whined. But the light was not guiding me to any sort of safety. For in that spotlight was pure horror, tremendously massive, something beyond my comprehension—the embodiment of Hell. Knotted like jungle vines, these thick vascular tubes lined with serrated polyps; all things twisting and contorting against one another. The light left and swiftly came back around to show me more of it. From its polyps grew faces and hands and feet; souls screaming in pain, writhing as they struggled so desperately to break through its fleshy membrane, to escape. And as the light moved, I witnessed the true expanse of it: a great serpent wall built from human flesh what wept a veneer of gluttony and oozed yellow puss from its pores—a great mass of the damned mulched and sewn together to form this entity, this storm.

I shrunk down the railing, convulsing, clutching my sanity with empty palms. "Turn it off!" I screamed. "Turn off the light!" For in the darkness, there was normality, emptiness; a void with no good nor bad. "God, Hugh, Alina, anybody, please…"

I took in a breath and shouted louder than I had ever done, screamed louder than I knew I could, like a dozen battle drums sounding in the deep or a horn bellowing at the fringe of war: "Turn off the light!"

Part 5

"..."

A deep note vibrated through my empty dreams until I woke.

Three leaks I now counted, drip-dropping from the ceiling.

With a pillow, I covered my ears to block out that drone which returned cyclically every thirty seconds, stretching loud and far into the otherwise silent morning. What was that? It was a horrendous, invasive and unignorable whine that consumed my senses. That's the damn foghorn; why in God's name was that thing on?

The events from last night began to unfold in stop motion within my mind. The last thing I remembered was... No, wait, that must have been a dream. There was no story to recount; no recollection of shutting down the lighthouse engine, walking back to the cottage nor crawling into bed.

I slid from my covers and braced against the frozen morning. I'd slept in my clothes, and despite being dressed, the cold was utterly unbearable. My limbs were unresponsive, my extremities numb. I was like a statue come to life, breaking free of its stone casing.

I pulled my overalls on top of my jumper and wore my lightkeeper coat above that, then laced my boots. When I looked up, I noticed that the black mould had spread across the wall. The circular patterns layered so thickly that they had evolved into one black mass; colonies connected to far out clusters by veins of green-yellow-browns, appearing to carry the supply of moisture, acting as rivers. Strange that at a certain angle, the mould looked three-dimensional, extending deep into the wall as if a tunnel. It was just a trick of the light, no doubt.

The wall, this canvass, was now a sprawl of spores riddled with the dregs of existence, and in it, I could not help but see the great cities of humanity; civilisation with our wretched pollution, dirt, miasmas and sin—an unholy writhing blight. I understood then that the Devil already had dominion over this world. Hell had come a long, long time ago at the very start of our journey. Hell came as soon as man picked rock from ground and carved branch to spear. If the world that I left was Hell, then what was this place I had come too?

Poised at my bedroom door, I huffed heat into my hands to thaw them so I could grasp the handle. The moisture from my breath instantly transformed into ice that fell slowly over my fingers. So, I pinched the cuffs of my woollen jumper to cover my palm and jimmied the handle down.

Frost had gathered inside the cottage and crunched under my boots. Daylight splintered into the hallway, not from windows but cracks and holes in the ceiling. Glass, plaster and brick—all manners of debris—collected into heaps as though a labour of moles had dug up through the floor.

The cottage had been devasted by the storm, yet I held no sentiment towards it.

"Hugh?" I mumbled.

In between the bass of the foghorn lay an eery quiet that hung about the place. Everything had frozen to a halt, and only my heartbeat, brothered to that haunting drone, persisted at the end of time.

"Hugh!" I shouted, knocking on his door. "Hugh? You in there?"

No reply, so I entered his room. The bed had been made, and there was no mess on the floor. I could see not one disturbance of life. The room was as dormant as I remembered it to be on my first day.

In the kitchen, the ceiling had caved in, the windows smashed, and the crockery lay shattered on the floor. The thick frost settled across everything and yet, on the dinner table, scrunched-up foil nestled the picked-clean fish bones, but I didn't hold this against Hugh. He needed the energy more than I for the trip to town. Besides, I had no appetite for food; it was far too cold.

There was no food and no water. No warmth, no life. It seemed as though God had abandoned me. Had I passed or failed this test? Had I failed *her*?

Before I could even begin to comprehend this new world, I needed to get warm.

In the burner, embers pulsed with the faintest of heats and coolest of reds smothered in grey ash. I picked up the poker and attempted to enrage the fire with fresh kindling. The ashen front dispersed, revealing something underneath that was not quite burnt—the remnants of a little book. Its leather covering was charred, and the lettering had seared off, but I knew this book. It was my wife's Bible.

I plunged my hand into the ash and picked out what remained of the book. I held the thing in my hand and carefully pulled the charred cover open. Even with the most delicate of touches, the interior disintegrated, and the dead matter powdered over me. It was gone. The words, the prayers, *her*—all turned to ash.

There was no inconsolable rage kindling inside me. No outburst of things thrown, smashed or fists slammed into walls. There was nothing inside me worth burning to produce such chaos, and neither did I desire it. I was frozen into submission.

I threw the remnants of the book back into the burner and crafted a fire. I felt somewhat weightless without it, free of shackles. If there were a gust, I would surely have floated away. However, the sensation did not stick. It was a cheap and fleeting high—a goddamned lie. That momentary incandescence reduced only to the most distant starlight, barely twinkling amidst the unfathomable black guilt.

I paused underneath the overhang by the front door, not knowing which direction to take. A haar had frozen to the air so thickly that it appeared to be a solid wall. I couldn't see three-foot in front of me. Eyes on my feet, I followed the path, using the drone of the foghorn to confirm my direction.

The foghorn sounded again, this time from behind me far away, though only moments ago it was in front of me, aligned with the pale light in the sky. I had not turned a full circle. I had not veered left or right even a fraction, I'm sure of it. I had only moved forward across the grass.

Agony in my ears as the foghorn howled; a catalyst to yet another throbbing migraine. After only five steps, the sound came again, impossibly close.

Now directly beside the foghorn tower, I shouted, "Hugh!" and again, "Hugh!"

The horn seemed to mimic me, drowning me out until I was just warm, wordless air.

From the tower, I edged towards the cliff with my hands clamped to my ears. The mist was thick across the bay. I could barely make out the start of the water, trickling and rising silently between the rocks, with the delicate weight of sheet ice breaking on its surface.

I trekked along the cliffside until I reached the slipway at the northernmost point of the island. I dropped down and walked to the waterline and —

There was the skiff, ruined, half-beached, half-sunk. Chunks of the wooden hull were strewn about the water. The ores were snapped in two, their halves gradually drifting away. I didn't know what I expected, but I wasn't surprised. Perhaps I'd even heard it unfold last night as I cowered in the lighthouse, or perhaps I saw it in one of my dreams; Hugh as the storm, two and the same, who in some incomprehensible act had devastated the skiff upon the rocks.

I was marooned.

My knees slammed into the concrete floor. I expelled my anguish in a long groan then gasped and cried for saltless water. My entire body shivered, desperate for heat, yet I would not pray. Parched into silence, I had no more words left for God.

I searched for the lighthouse. I could see it shine blueish through the mist, but I never found it; neither here nor there, and always the same distance away, never closer.

My shadow walked at my heels with misaligned footsteps. Disturbances swirled in the periphery of fog, watching me, haunting me. Distant calls of beasts from the deep echoed, and sirens whispered close in familiar voices. It was her voice: "Rob."

"Alina?" I spoke. "Is that you? Alina, please, I—"

The whisper came again, this time it was Hugh thundering in my ear. "Robert."

I spun around and threw a savage right hook into the outline of Hugh's face — an outline which instantly dissolved into the mist, with the plume of his breath floating away on the breeze.

"Where are you, Devil?" I called out.

I stopped through no will of my own. I could not move. Roots that I could not see fastened me to this position. Then, out from the blinding white, a pale arm snatched me, grasped my neck and squeezed with a mechanical grip as rough as rope, tightening around my bare skin. Those feminine hands started to peel, blacken, then seared into my flesh.

Life was dragged away from me. Memories collapsed under their heavy, tangible meaning and burst through to the present where they overlapped and confused. She was skewing my mind.

With a wild smack, I knocked the arm away from me and fell to the ground. My feet were still routed, so I slipped off the boots and crawled a quick distance, pushing myself to my feet. I ran across the stones; stones that quickly turned into shards of ice, stabbing. With force, I thudded into the door of the cottage.

I glanced back at the swirling fog. The whispers were still out there, calling for me, calling for my soul. Then, in a sudden gust, the presence returned, surging towards me from the mist. I closed the door and turned the lock, bracing against it with my back. Thumps and kicks hammered relentlessly, and the handle bounced in its fixings. Slam. Slam. Slam... Then, it stopped.

The whispers came again, gently to my ears, seductively, then soured into vicious, hateful screams. The calls subsided into a constant sob — it was Alina.

"Please. Rob, please. I need you, Rob. Help me... You did this. You did this to me. You put me in this place!"

It took everything to resist the cries of my dead wife.

Eventually, the ghosts stopped, and I abandoned my post. I needed to reset myself.

The daylight coming through the stunt bathroom window constructed a ghoulish image in the mirror. Neither real nor living, I was the colour of grey — in between. My body had deteriorated. I had felt the cramping pains of dehydrated organs and been aware of the shrinking muscles, though I'd not thought my famine to be this severe. I only ate yesterday, at least that is what I perceived. Yet what I saw was a man on the brink of starvation, who'd not drank water since...

I wore a swollen gut, hung upon a skeletal frame. The corners of my shoulders stuck out from their fleshy wrappings. My clavicles were like elevated suspension bridges, covered only by a water-thin lacquer of skin. I caressed the ridges and the valleys between my ribcage. I dug my thumbs into the gorges of my sunken cheeks. I'd become something wretched, a scorned creature, a castaway.

Glancing down, I saw my hands. These hands I studied before pushing them through bedraggled hair. Fingers that then combed through this beard and followed a sharp jawline to the chin which dented inwards. These hands, shaking, moved to the neck and felt the burn mark left from her grip, then jittered along the shoulders and down the chest, tracing the lines of bones where I didn't remember them to be; this wasn't my body.

I could not believe my deep-set yellowed eyes. It was a nasty trick of the light.

I twisted the sink taps; no water. So, I licked my index fingers and dabbed them into my eyes. The saliva hurt, no, burned like alcohol. My eyelids retracted, and the blurriness faded, revealing, "Hugh?" He was staring right back at me, smiling wide, grinning teeth with cheeks pulled tight over bone. "That's not possible." It was Hugh, but It was also me. Yes, we were similar in height, build, features, but he was never me. He was never me! "Give it back!" I shouted. "You've got my face. Give it back!" I punched the mirror. "Give it back!" I hit the glass again, and on the third strike, the pane shattered, splintering into my knuckles. "You're a liar, Hugh! You took her from me. You can go to Hell! You can—" Exhaustion took my breath away, took my emotion from me. And I crashed into a calm, scrunching foetal on the floor amongst fractured glass.

*

In my bedroom, clutching to the very seams of my sight, was the man with the light in his mouth, puffing smoke and breathing. It was something more than a reflection of myself. It had been there this whole time—a shadow watching me from my past nailed to my present. This ghost I saw out the corner of my eye then became entangled by the undulating black mould on the wall, which reached with spined arms pulling my past self into the endless dark where it feasted on my inner rot.

I lumbered lifelessly down the hallway, scrapping my feet along the ground as I went. Debris mounded to my ankles, and the state of the cottage had worsened with time. How much time, exactly? It was as if twenty years had passed since I came back inside the cottage to shelter from the screams.

I stumbled into the living room and knelt in front of the burner, desperately reaching in for some heat. Tough, charred leather buried under cinder—what had Hugh been burning?

I scooped up a handful of warm ash and smothered it across my face. A flutter of joy, of hope, sparked inside me as

I felt the heat loosen my rigid skin. It didn't last, and the heat faded as quickly as it came. I went to scoop another handful of warm ash, but the embers had gone.

Cold again.

There was no furniture in the room. There was only the burner and—slam—behind me now was a chest; the same one where I found the fishing rod. It opened without me touching it, and I saw its contents without viewing them. Underneath the folds of dusty blankets, these hands gripped the barrel of steel with a sureness, as though I knew what it was and how to use it. A sense of determination swept through me, wave by wave, stronger and stronger until I could stand. Blood flowed. Energy kindled movement.

I realised what had to be done.

It wasn't ghosts screaming at the door this time, but the thunderous storm with winds whirring, howling like a choir of wolves. And that drone of the foghorn sounded ever-louder, so tremendously close that it shook the building—the horn of war, God's trumpet, calling me to the close.

My mind was a mess of thoughts, memories, feelings and horrors, colliding past and future, fiction and not. Stammering and quaking, I paused on the verge of utter implosion and scrambled for these pieces of me, vaguely clutching my sanity to my chest before stepping outside.

At that moment, the fog lifted, and the day phased into darkness.

Underneath the overhang, shaking, I courted a lit matchstick to a cigarette and spied on the lantern room. As usual, Hugh had locked himself in there with *her*, with the light. I could see him seducing her, tainting her with his sin. He'd been in her ear each night, spreading his venom, laying his vermin.

I walked past the lighthouse and towards the centre of the island. I wandered aimlessly across the grass until I came to the barn where I was meant to be. Inside, the place stank, with petrol splashed up the walls and drizzled in lines like slug trails; this was more than enough.

And the fumes ignited before the match could reach the ground, exploding into a fireball that burst inches above my head. I ducked and scurried to the exit, outracing the spread of orange preceded by blue. It took only minutes for the entire barn to catch alight.

I waited in front of the barn. The heat kept the cold from me, warmed my bones and soul until I was almost human again. Though with fire comes smoke, and my throat started to fill with it.

I continued to wait.

Finally, she noticed and fixed her light upon me. It was working. This was it.

Hugh's shadow dashed across her gaze as he left the lantern room. He was—clunk, clunk, clunk—trotting down the metal stairs. I could hear: the drones of the engine room as he moved past, the open and close of the lighthouse door, his footsteps along the gravel path, the rustling of grass, his creaking joints, the inhales, exhales, the rise and fall of his chest, and his heartbeat quickening.

Hugh slowed, edging towards me from the crawling blackness.

"Come into the light!" I demanded, and he did, shielding his eyes from the blaze.

"What happened, Rob? Are you okay?" he panted. Here he stood, the manifestation of my evils, the rot within me, this time looking much less like myself as I saw him now, less like what the mirror had shown me. A man in his own right, yet an illusion nonetheless—a devilish trick. "You okay?"

"I know what you are, Hugh," I said, "the godless poison inside of me. The faithless odour and the doubtful mannequin of what I was. But she will see it: that I am worthy of forgiveness."

I raised the rifle.

"You don't have to do this-you don't-it's not what I meant it's-forgive yourself, not this. Not this."

"My past is my tether to this place. And you're just another shade of what I was. But I am changed."

I almost thought he was real as the emotion rippled through him, contorting into realisation, anger and then true, undeniable fear.

"Don't... Rob."

It was instant. The crackle of thunder. The boom of another wave striking the cliffside. A gaping mouth and a hole filled with brilliant light. A smile underneath a red fountain.

I expected my redemption to rush through me, stampeding like cattle at the sound of gunfire. I expected a heavy and present pounding as I filled with life once again, as normality took hold and my future surged from murky depths. Instead, there came an off-beat palpitation throbbing in my throat, wrists, along my arms and the backs of my legs. Everything inside me became stretched into a freefall, warped by that sensation, of the gravity of it, of the severe permeance of it. I'd not expected the blood splatter, the pink matter of brain or the exaggerated exit hole of his blown-out skull. I didn't imagine the twitching of the corpse or the expression, somewhere between begging and terror, to stain his face as he lay there bloodening the grass. What gripped me then, that feeling that lingered in the furthest corners of my being, was doubt; doubt of whether I'd truly changed.

I dropped the rifle and scraped the blood from my beard. My trial had not yet finished.

I staggered towards the lighthouse, past the engine room and bumbled up the stairs. When exhaustion hit, I crawled on my hands and knees. When my knees gave way, I used my arms to haul my weight, step by step, with the very last of my resolve. I couldn't have been far from death itself, but even then, I did not pray.

I climbed through the hatch into the lantern room, and there she was: "Alina." My wife, my beacon, bursting through the darkness.

I fell onto her, smothering the lens in red motor oil, in blood, and I kissed her. "Forgive me," I said, and I kept repeating it: "Forgive me. Forgive me. Forgive me."

I reached underneath the lens and gripped the bulb, with one hand fastened around the neck, squeezing. The light was warm, welcoming. I never thought I would be able to hold her again unless I made it to Heaven; is that where I was, holding her heat, her love, so close?

I was almost there, back in the kitchen, eating food at the table together just talking about things, about life and futures and nothing, baked in a Summer's Sunday evening sun filtering through the voile curtains, patterning the room into vague florals furling almost like morning mists or moving breaths pushing hot into cold. Her cooking, her voice, her smile, tattooed on my mind, imprinted as phosphenes across my memories, always there, lingering in the dark whenever I closed my eyes. Neither living nor dead, but somewhere in between, both bound to eternal suffering on this island, in this purgatory.

The glass began to crack under the pressure.

"I have suffered willingly, and I stand here changed. I know this. I have no doubt that I am not the monster I was. I have vanquished my Devil; the evil who wore my face and raged like the storm. This is me now, do you see me? Whoever is watching—the light, my Lord, my wife, my own

122

reflection—see that I am changed. I am ready for my forgiveness, and I will take it."

I smashed the lantern in my hand—

But the light did not go out. The glass shattered and the filament snapped, yet a vengeful brightness remained, as hot as the sun, with hands of flames reaching for my soul. I smiled amidst the fire, burning, screaming, "Grant me my redemption."

...

I awaited light to overcome the darkness. I awaited my baptism, my forgiveness. But the relief never came. The coruscation dimmed into deep vermillion, and there rose a smell of rotten, putrid things, followed by the cacophony of an unending storm, of fathomless ocean swells, heavy rain and screeching metal engines. Yet, above everything, I heard the cascading madness of all peoples as they fell forever across the verge of nowhere.

Afterword

"I think it's time you stop this writing business and get a real job."

Not too long after she said that, my Grandma died.

So here's to her. Here's to the ghost of her eating those words. Maybe she'd be impressed, what do you think? I like to think that anyway. Ever since she said it, I couldn't wait to prove her wrong, but it had to be the right story, the right words, the best I could do. But those words came too late. And maybe she'd have absolutely hated my story, maybe not, but at least she would have read it.

In the end, I got the job she wanted me to get. I never stopped writing though—three hours a day, and maybe one of these days I'll write something worth mine and your time. So, if you got this far, I both sincerely thank you and apologise. If I misplaced a comma, overused a semi-colon, post me some feedback and I'll take it on board... Well, at least until I can afford a professional editor anyway.

*

Back to the story, however, and for those that read this and thought "what a rip-off of The Lighthouse" directed by Robert Eggers, well get lost, finders keepers shut up. I don't care. I totally had the idea first; Back in 2017, in fact, after reading a LadBible article on the sale of 'Your Very Own Private Island'—Little Ross Island that is, complete with a lighthouse situated just off the Southwest Coast of Scotland.

I wrote the original short story for a university module on historical writing. I remember declaring in my critical write-up that this would be the perfect idea for a movie and that I should write the script before someone beats me to it. The Lighthouse movie was released in 2019… Martin, did you sell my idea? That movie was based on the famous Smalls Lighthouse Tragedy, similar to the true story I had found, but different nonetheless.

The characters Robert and Hugh were real Lightkeepers who worked together on Little Ross Island in 1960. Rob killed Hugh with a .22 Rifle, and nobody knows why. It is heavily speculated that Rob may have had a mental condition. After the body was discovered, there was a nationwide manhunt for Rob. When he was found, he was sentenced to hang; this was commuted to life in prison, no doubt partly due to his mental instability. Rob later took his own life in jail.

Duality was my poster boy theme for the story which went hand in hand with the cyclic nature of the plot journey. From the bipolar weather, role-reversal dialogue, drip-drop leaks to the two main characters, Robert and Hugh, so similar but different; two sides of a grimy coin. However, the real duality of the piece comes with my attempt to write the conclusion of the story in such a way that Rob's fate could be interpreted differently. A believer might see a story of a man failing the trials of God, thus descending into Hell, and a non-believer could easily decide that Rob had lost his mind and had slipped into insanity, like so many Lightkeepers before him. *This is all stuff I hoped to achieve, whether I did achieve that... Well, that's up to you to decide.*

There were three undertows of madness dragging the plot forward to its close. The first was mental instability, and as you can tell, if you read it, I was inspired by the 'real' Rob. At first, I introduced this theme in the world-building: weather, sea, temperature, light vs dark and then in Rob's mood swings. I heightened the visuals to try and disguise any trace of the mental illness theme until Part 4 when things started to get weird. And as we see, Rob's condition worsens to a likened state of split-personality, displacing his inner evils, his past sins, as Hugh.

The next undertow is that of religious downfall or failure. I have no idea if Rob was religious in real life, but I wanted a second overt theme to separate my work from Robert Eggars' *The Lighthouse*. The island, doubling as a metaphor for Rob's internal torment, was written as a purgatory, cast in black and white; a greyed place sat between the mainland and the boundless ocean. The island is an in-between zone, just like purgatory, and it is here he awaited judgement or his 'redemption' from God. And Hugh, this supposed reflection of Rob's past, would therefore be his final test.

Ultimately, Robert failed God's test. He had not changed. He repeated the cycle of doubt and rage once again, killing the beacon just as he did his wife; as cyclic as the sound of the foghorn, the rotation of the light, the inhales and exhales of cigarette smoke, of tobacco addiction, and as constant as the seas boring into the cliffside. He is doomed to repeat his terrible secret over and over, with his past as ever-present as persistent mould, festering, benign yet malignant on the horizon, a stagnant storm that returns each night with such reckless rage—this is Rob's Hell.

And the third theme—and if you got it hats-off—was madness through mercury poisoning. Mercury is used to float the beacon on the rotator mechanism in place of water because it is a denser liquid. Mercury needed to be cleaned/replaced every so often, which exposed unknowing Lightkeepers to the deadly vapours. It is theorised that the reason Keepers often went mad was due to mercury poisoning. Mercury vapour rots your brain with common symptoms being headaches, tremors, anxiety, depression, irritability, insomnia numbness, emotional instability and memory problems—all are subtly present in the story.

The novella has taken me about six months to write, re-write, edit and proof. The original novella I finished in July and was set in modern times based around a family who bought the lighthouse after a tragedy. Twenty-five-thousand words this was (1/3 of a full novel), which I scrapped after reading through. Why? Well, I wasn't even using the most powerful part of the story for a start, the fact that it happened in real life! Why in the Hell did I not start with that? There were also far too many characters for the narrow and claustrophobic feel of the story, and a botched, overly visible sense of horror. The phrase 'Murder your darlings' comes to mind. The original just didn't work, and the horror elements were abstract and random, and so visible they did not inspire fear, merely displayed it which takes away from the whole point of horror. As H.P. Lovecraft said:

"The oldest and strongest emotion of mankind is fear, and the oldest and strongest kind of fear is fear of the unknown."

For those that are interested, there are a few nods to Lovecraftian horror throughout the piece which I'm sure you already noticed. There are other themes, metaphors and meanings interlaced within the story that I have not covered and that you might not have detected, for example, time dilation. But at the risk of over-explaining myself, which I've probably already done no doubt, I implore you to read a second time; I've been told its worth it.

Every time I come to the page, I question my abilities, my work, the sentence I wrote yesterday that makes absolutely no sense... Wait, or does it? You should put a comma there, oh, no, wait you shouldn't put a comma there. No actually yeah put a comma there... I've come to the conclusion that nothing I ever write will be perfect, and that knocked my pride. The best course of action is to accept the flaws and get my work in front of eyes: your eyes. You may hate it or love it. You might never read my work again and throw your e-book into the fire, but if you enjoyed even one slither of my writing, just one morsel, a sentence, then I can walk away with a smile on my face—I did my job.

Yours Begrudgingly,

K. Daniel Crow

About the Author

I am a Birmingham-based UK writer with over half a decade's experience writing badly, sure, and writing exceptionally...Well, that's up to you to decide. I have previously been published in short story anthologies and have written six complete novels, of which still need to be edited (at some point).

I specialise in the weird, the psychological and the mind-bending, with atmospheric worlds and vivid imagery of which your eyes to gorge upon. My commitment to you, my readers, is to produce as close to a moving picture in your heads as possible, like a film, but with deeper meaning and greater insight.

What else? Uhm… I don't live at home with my cats or dogs like every other author seems to. I'm about as edgy as a candle, and I like listening to dark atmospheric soundtracks whilst I write.

I hope you enjoy my worlds!